EJ
Rodge
Rodgers & Hammerstein

My Favorite Things

MY FAVORITE THINGS

RODGERS & HAMMERSTEIN'S

My Favorite Things

ILLUSTRATED BY

RENÉE GRAEF

HarperCollins*Publishers*

My Favorite Things

Text copyright © 1959 by Richard Rodgers and Oscar Hammerstein II

Copyright renewed by Williamson Music, owner of publication and allied rights throughout the world.

International copyright secured. All rights reserved. Reprinted by permission. Illustrations copyright © 2001 by Renée Graef.

Manufactured in China. For information address HarperCollins Children's Books,

a division of HarperCollins Publishers, 1350 Avenue of the Americas, New York, NY 10019.

ISBN 0-06-028710-1 — ISBN 0-06-029233-4 (lib. bdg.) — ISBN 0-06-443627-6 (pbk.)

www.harperchildrens.com   Typography by Carla Weise

❖ First Edition

For stepparents who guide and nurture their children with love,

especially Maria von Trapp and my own mother Louise

—RG

Raindrops on roses
and whiskers on kittens,

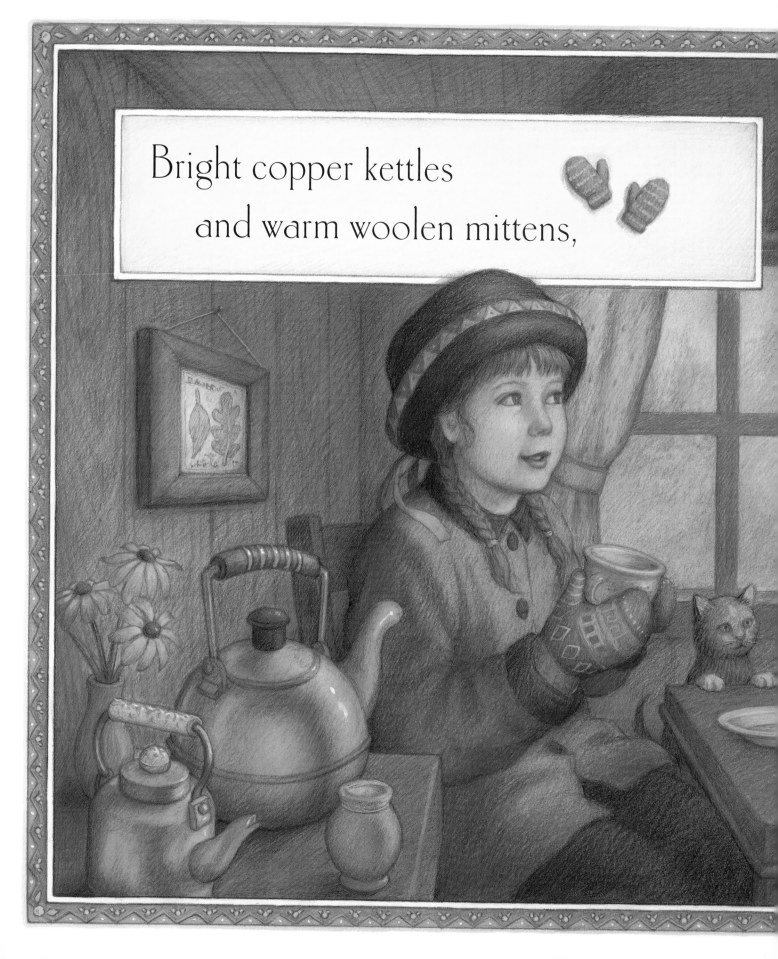

Bright copper kettles
and warm woolen mittens,

Brown paper packages
tied up with strings,

These are a few of my favorite things.

Cream-colored ponies
and crisp apple strudels,

Doorbells and sleighbells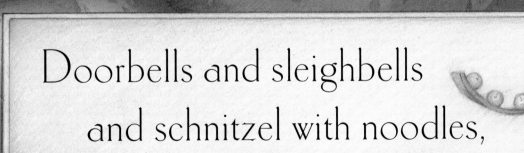
and schnitzel with noodles,

Wild geese that fly with
the moon on their wings,

These are a few of my favorite things.

Girls in white dresses
with blue satin sashes,

Snowflakes that stay
on my nose and eyelashes,

Silver white winters that melt into springs,

These are a few of my favorite things.

When the dog bites,
When the bee stings,
When I'm feeling sad,

I simply remember my favorite things
And then I don't feel so bad.

MY FAVORITE THINGS

Lyrics by OSCAR HAMMERSTEIN II
Music by RICHARD RODGERS

Rain-drops on roses and whisk-ers on kit-tens, Bright cop-per

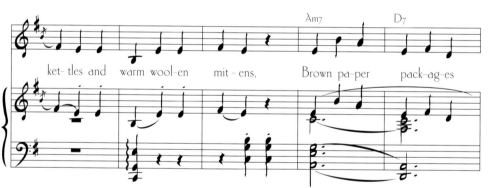

ket-tles and warm wool-en mit-ens, Brown pa-per pack-ag-es

tied up with strings, These are a few of my fa-vor-ite things.

When I'm feel - ing sad,_____ I

sim-ply re - mem-ber my fa - vor - ite things and

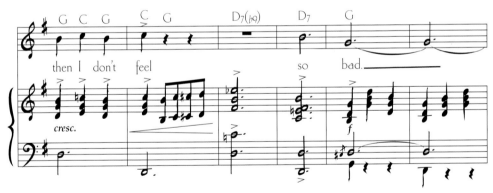

then I don't feel so bad._____

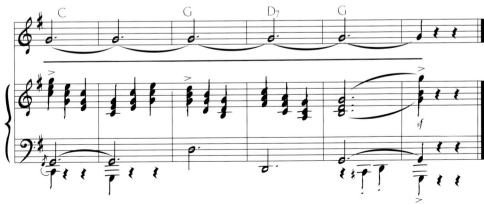